DECK THE SANTA

A MURDER ALL THE WAY CHRISTMAS COZY MYSTERY (BOOK 1)

SUE HOLLOWELL

CONTENTS

CHAPTER ONE

I plunked my bag on the floor, backed my legs to the edge of the bed, and flopped backwards. Max hopped up and did the same, placing his snout on my thigh. The drive up to Hollywerth with Mom and Max spanned half a day. I needed to pace my energy for this trip. A family reunion wasn't at the top of my list, but Mom insisted we all get together for an adventure. Truth be told, every day with her was an adventure. Since my return to Cedarbrook to help her run the treehouse hotel, we had become closer than ever. In her eight plus decades on the planet, that woman lived her life to the fullest. And the tiniest bit had rubbed off on me.

"Chloe, are you going to take a nap?" she piped up, flinging open the curtains.

My body said yes, but I was sure Mom had other plans. I would have to find the coffee shop and goose up my energy with some caffeine. "No. Just catching my breath."

Max shifted his eyes toward me and then over toward Mom. I pointed in her direction, and he leaped off the bed, reaching his front paws to the windowsill. His stubby tail circled like a propeller. He glanced back at me. His big brown eyes beckoned me to join them.

Hollywerth was a Bavarian village that went full out for Christmas every year. I stepped to Mom's right side, looped my arm around her waist and squeezed. Snow covered everything and tiny flakes drifted aimlessly toward the ground. My expectations for our family visit were tempered, but I tried to keep my mind open to the magic of the place and season. Christmas lights lined the buildings, sure to brighten the night when lit. They prepared the towering evergreen tree in the town square for the upcoming lighting ceremony. My arms prickled with goosebumps. This venue really took you away to a festive time. We had planned several days here, hopefully plenty of time to take in all the town offered. I had already spotted several things inspiring me to expand our activities at the hotel back home. Birding trips. Horseback rides. Maybe even a fishing contest at our little lake. I enjoyed planning the events almost as much as our guests enjoyed attending.

Turning to face the room, I questioned booking the suite. The treehouse hotel was doing well and holding its own financially, but I still bristled at large purchases. The space suited part of our purpose for the trip. An expansive conference table consumed half of the room, with a nearby small kitchen. I didn't think you could get more adventurous than going into business with family. Mom and I running the hotel was one thing, but both of my sisters and brother in partnership for a restaurant? That signaled I had completely lost my mind.

Trying not to get myself overwhelmed by thinking too far ahead about family stuff, I said, "What about we head to the lobby and check out the schedule of events?"

Max slid from the windowsill and marched directly to Mom's bag on the floor. With one paw, he nudged it onto its side. A miniature gnome, adorned in Christmas garb like an elf, toppled out.

Mom scurried to it and scooped it up. "Max, leave that alone!"

How that dog always found the gnomes was beyond me. He had a love-hate relationship with them, mostly hate, and I could never figure out why.

"Is that-?"

"Yes, Chloe," was all Mom said. She placed the gnome next to the television and lifted her bag to the table.

I suspected there was much more to the story that I wasn't ready to hear. "Maybe we should unpack a bit, then we can go explore," I said.

Mom clapped her hands. It warmed my heart to see her so happy. And not much gave her the level of joy of all her kids together. Not having kids myself, I didn't quite understand that. We had certainly gotten off to a rocky start when I had agreed for a temporary return to Cedarbrook to help with the hotel. I couldn't have imagined how my life would change with that decision.

Max perched himself on a side chair as mom and I wheeled our suitcases to the dresser. "Mom, why do you have so much luggage?" If my calculations were even close, she had enough for weeks as opposed to days.

With a dismissive wave, she said, "I wasn't sure what to pack. Just wanted to be prepared."

There were a variety of activities both inside and out in the snowy weather. But even double what I had wouldn't fill the number of suitcases she brought.

"Do you know what you want to do yet?" I asked, settling back on the bed to wait for her to finish.

"Everything."

I reached for my purse, retrieving the brochure that our travel agent friend had provided. Opening it up, I ran my finger down the list of amenities, way too many for the time we had. Maybe a return trip another year.

"OK. When we get to the lobby, we can see what's still available." I tapped the paper. "They have a photo opp with Santa for dogs."

Max tipped his head slightly, ears flopping. The little golden cocker spaniel was my constant companion. Would he sit still enough to get a picture? Hollywerth would be quite the adventure for him, too. I only hoped he wasn't too tempted by all the new experiences. The birds, the reindeer who pulled the sleigh, and certainly all the kids.

"I'm thinking at least the tree lighting, the Santa visit. And then I'm game for what anyone else wants to do," I said.

Mom shoved the drawer closed, stuffing the clothes down to squeeze it shut. "I really want to see the nutcracker museum. Can you believe they have a museum of just nutcrackers?" She grinned as I tried to read between the lines of her comment. "Let's check the hours on our way to the lobby."

I marveled at her energy and ability to follow her own path without caring what others thought. We grabbed our purses and left the room. Christmas music softly filled the hallway as we headed to the elevators. Mom tucked her arm under my elbow and leaned her head on me. The elevator dinged, and we entered, Max dutifully sitting by my side. That dog had more manners than some people.

Standing back, Mom said, "Oh, and that coffee shop, too."

Also highlighted in the marketing materials was Jules' Cafe, boasting a large variety of Bavarian desserts. Maybe Mom was onto something, packing a few extra clothes. I may have made a mistake in not packing more stretchy pants. My friend from Cedarbrook who owned Caroline's Confections had sent me on a mission to scout out any new must-have items she might add to her menu. That would be a tough mission, but one I was prepared to take on.

The elevator deposited us into a hallway leading to the lobby. I saw from where we stood that a long line had formed at the check-in counter.

"Max," I said, hoping he got my drift to stay by my side, reconsidering the leash back in our room.

"Chloe, look." Mom had stopped at a window of the nutcracker museum. Her hand shaded her eyes. "Looks like they're closed for inventory of the gift shop." She pointed to a sign on the door.

"OK. Well, we've got time. We can come back later."

"Hello ladies," said a woman approaching from the lobby, her name tag read Anabel.

CHAPTER TWO

nabel's shoulder-length, curly brown hair bounced with her step. She retrieved keys from her pocket and inserted one into the lock, peering through the glass. "We're opening in about an hour if my crew is on schedule. And who is this guy?" Anabel kneeled and reached to scratch Max's ears. He glanced at me as I nodded permission. Max's snout plunged straight into Anabel's pocket, retrieving a gingersnap. He moved back, grinning.

"I'm so sorry. Those are his weakness." I tugged Max's collar. "I'll pay you for that."

Waving me off, Anabel said, "No worries. Jules has tons of these, especially this time of year."

Max quickly inhaled the little cookie, extending his paw to tap my knee. *Yes, little buddy, I got the message. We will stop by to see Jules.*

Mom returned to the window, scanning the interior. "Chloe, we have to come back. Just look." She stepped back, pointing at the floor-to-ceiling displays of the nutcrackers. Who knew there were so many varieties, enough to have an official museum?

"If you want, I can give you just a quick peek. But we can't disturb the inventory process. I really need that to finish soon. As you can imagine, this is our busiest time of year." Anabel turned the key in the lock and swung the door open.

Leading the way, Max stopped just inside the door, surveying the room. I wondered if the nutcrackers looked too close to the garden gnomes he usually toyed with. Mom and Max had a running feud with those little characters.

"Max," I said as his rear moved side to side. Yep, his wheels were already turning.

Anabel moved past us as we stood gazing all around. A return visit was in order.

"I'm getting an idea, Chloe," Mom said, approaching a wall displaying special museum pieces. These were truly a work of art. The walnut and ivory swashbuckling pirate was carved in France from one piece of walnut except the handle. His jacket was dotted with ivory studs. And his hat even had an ivory feather.

"Lloyd," came a scream from Anabel toward the back of the museum.

Max took off like a shot in the direction of Anabel. Mom and I looked at each other. What in the world did Lloyd do? I imagined you need to be super careful with the nutcrackers, some of them dating back centuries. Hopefully, the disaster wasn't something they couldn't recover from.

Returning to us, bouncing up and down, Max pivoted and took several steps toward Anabel. Hmmm. He wanted me to follow him. Was he concerned with Anabel's tone? I followed his lead. "Mom, I'll be right back. Then we need to go."

"Sure, dear," she mumbled.

I rounded the corner to find Anabel slumped on the floor over Santa. I knelt next to her and saw a man in the full jolly guy suit. "Is he?" I asked.

Sniffling, Anabel nodded and wailed, dropping herself across the body.

Max whimpered as he stood on the opposite side of big red. My sensitive boy. His left front paw edged forward toward the object of his focus. An open bag of gingersnap cookies, one of them half eaten.

Shaking my head, I made a note to get him some treats later. I couldn't remember when his obsession with the cookies started, but he was hooked. I placed my hand on Anabel's back as her body shuddered.

Without Anabel answering my question, I knew the response. Quietly, I said, "We need to report this."

Anabel sat back on her heels and scanned the room. She tipped her head, continuing to look around. I mimicked her gesture, unsure of what she was looking for. Other than Santa splayed on the floor next to a broken nutcracker, and some cookie crumbles, nothing appeared out of place. She placed her hands on the floor and hoisted herself up.

A gasp from behind us prompted us all to turn in unison. "What happened? Is he OK?" Mom asked.

I stepped between her and the body, closing my eyes and shaking my head. A quick glance over my shoulder, I whispered, "We need to go to the lobby." Patting my leg, I said, "Max."

Dutifully, my boy joined us as he stared at Anabel.

Mom said, "I'll go, Chloe. You stay here." She pointed at Lloyd. "Such a shame. Who will the kids visit now at Santa's Workshop?"

Who indeed? Anabel glanced up as Mom exited. "I hadn't even thought of that."

That was the least of our worries. This poor man was dead, and it looked like someone had done him in. But why? Had he just been nibbling gingersnaps when someone struck him from behind with a prized nutcracker? It didn't seem like he should have been eating as he went about his work with these collectibles.

Anabel stooped to reach for the broken nutcracker on the floor.

"Stop!" I knew more about crime scenes than I wanted to, and rule number one was touch nothing. I lowered my voice. "I'm sorry." Gently touching Anabel's elbow, I guided her to the doorway. "We probably shouldn't disturb anything until someone can take a look."

"But I've got to open soon. It's one of the biggest times of the year." No doubt crowds arriving in Hollywerth for the annual Christmas activities would flood the museum. However, not today.

"We Wish You a Merry Christmas" softly emanated from the ceiling speakers, in stark contrast to the scene in front of us. I draped my left arm around Anabel's shoulders and Max gingerly leaned against her left leg.

I dared to ask the obvious question. "Do you know anyone who would want to hurt Lloyd?"

"No," she squeaked.

Did she not know, or was she covering for some reason? Leaving a lengthy, awkward silence allowed her to continue.

"I mean, Greg wasn't happy when Lloyd got the job this year," Anabel said.

Now we were talking. "Why was there a change?" If I could prompt some initial answers before Mom came back, we might have a suspect identified.

"Looks like Greg will have his old job back," Anabel mumbled. She crouched and placed her hand on Santa's, glancing back at me, tears flowing. Was there more to this relationship than employer, employee? Certainly, finding a dead body would shock anyone, and you couldn't predict someone's behavior in dire circumstances.

"Right here," came Mom's voice from behind us. We all took a few steps back so the concierge could see the center of attention.

"Oh, boy," she said. "Anabel, I'm so sorry." Holding her arm out to keep us away from the body, she continued, "I radioed the police."

Anabel whipped her head around. The song piping into the room instructed us to have "A Holly Jolly Christmas."

A voice crackled over the walkie-talkie of the concierge. She unhooked it from her waistband and stepped from the room. Hushed voices prevented us from hearing what was no doubt a re-cap of a dead body in the nutcracker museum. And not just anyone, but Santa. Mom was right. There would be a lot of last-minute scrambling to recover. Only a mere few hours in Hollywerth and we were already smack-dab in the middle of a murder.

CHAPTER THREE

I touched Mom's arm and flicked my head toward the door. No reason for us to stay. I stepped forward to the concierge and whispered, "I'm Chloe Carson. Let us know if you need any information. We're in room 325." I suspected the police would pay us a visit, if only for additional background information on the discovery of the body. Mom, Max, and I filed from the room to the hallway.

"Well, that didn't go as planned," Mom said.

No, it did not. She got her peek into the museum but much more than we bargained for. I couldn't fathom how that would disrupt the Christmas festivities, although they likely had a Santa replacement in the wings. I took Mom's hand and led her to the lobby. We needed to regroup.

There wasn't a spot in the room not covered in holiday decorations. Beautiful evergreen wreaths with red bows adorned the fireplace mantel. I turned, "Mom."

"I know, Chloe. That really put a crimp in our day. But not as much as it did for Lloyd," she said, plopping into an overstuffed chair in front of the fireplace. I took the seat on the other side of a table between us that held a lamppost with a snowman leaning up against it. His rosy cheeks and smile beckoned me towards holiday cheer. Max hopped up next to me, rotating in a circle and plunking half of his body onto my thigh.

"Well, at least it seems like they've got an experienced Santa ready to step in," I said. How in the world did someone get into the locked museum and crack Santa over the head? Who would have access to the room? And why would they do that?

"What a cute dog," said the older woman seated across from us. As she stood, I could see her dressed in a teal t-shirt covered by a fluffy, pink, fur coat. Her head was wrapped in a matching teal bandanna, topping her golden-tinted glasses. What a character. "May I pet him?" she asked, reaching her arm toward Max.

His sharp elbow gouged my thigh as he stood to greet her. "Of course," I said.

"I'm Maude," she said. "Did I overhear something about Santa drama?"

Looking at Mom, I hesitated to spread news that wasn't mine to share. "I'm Chloe. This is my mom, Mabel." I tilted my head in Mom's direction. "And Max." I ran my hand down his back. If he were a cat, his purr would be rumbling loudly.

Maude scratched under his floppy ears. "Nice to meet you. Where are you from?"

"Cedarbrook," I said.

"Wait. Is that where those treehouses are?" Maude took a step back.

Nodding, I smiled.

"Oh, I have to visit sometime," Maude said. "That sounds right up my alley."

"Do you have a grandchild here?" Mom asked, pointing to the gaming device in Maude's hand.

Holding it out, she chuckled. "This? No. It's mine."

Mom and I exchanged looks. I wouldn't know what to do with one of those things, even if I had weeks of training. Max and I liked our pencil-and-paper puzzles just fine.

"Mabel, they have a game room. You should join me," Maude offered.

Standing, Mom said, "Oh no. I'm too old for that stuff."

"Nonsense. You're only as old as you decide to be." The game made several sounds, prompting Maude to look at the screen. "Ah nuts. I better put this on pause, or I'm going to lose my standing."

Max hopped to the floor, and following his lead, I stood. "Mom, why don't we see what's still available on the activity schedule?" I glanced toward a table near the concierge desk with a big board that held the daily schedule. A darling elf sat behind the table, chatting up those in line. Her head bobbed with the green and red hat atop her gray hair.

"Well," Mom said, moving to stand next to Maude. She wasn't seriously considering the game room, was she? Technology and she didn't get along very well. They still maintained the books at the hotel on paper when I arrived in Cedarbrook to help her out. She had agreed to automate, but only if I took care of that part. Deal.

"Why don't we sign up for what we want to do, then you can go with Maude," I said, wondering if I now had a teenager on my hands. My mother constantly surprised me. She had long since passed the time when she cared about what others thought of her. What a more peaceful way to live your life.

Mom held up her finger to Maude, signaling she would momentarily return to venture off to the game room. I was a little surprised that Hollywerth had accommodated an indoor activity like that, given all the holiday events held outdoors. I guessed they wanted to offer a variety of things for everyone.

As we approached the elf, Max hurried around the table to get a full view of her. I wondered if costumes threw him off a bit, unsure what this odd-looking character might do.

"Welcome to Hollywerth. What can I sign you up for?" The elf's name tag said Sherrie.

"Hi, Sherrie. I'm Chloe; this is my mom Mabel. And Max." I pointed to my boy, who sat staring at the elf.

"We have Santa's workshop that does pictures with pets," she said. Max swung his head toward me, grinning.

"OK. I think we have a winner." We'd see when we actually arrived at another person in costume if Max still felt the same.

Sherrie pointed to several pieces of paper in front of her. "Some of these require a sign up since there are limited spots. Others you can just show up."

"Mom." I turned to find her gazing off toward Maude. Teenage brain indeed. I only hoped by the time the rest of our family arrived, she could focus on the business at hand. It might first take her getting the gaming out of her system. I needed to make an executive decision. "Let's do a sleigh ride." I wrote our names into a slot on the paper.

"That's a good choice. We have actual reindeer to pull it," Sherrie added.

"I think for now, just the gingerbread house decorating contest," I said. Max sprinted from behind the table and put his paw near the sign-up sheet. Would my gingersnap loving pup be able to behave himself around all of that sweetness?

Approaching from across the lobby, Anabel came and whispered into Sherrie's ear. Sherrie shook her head, tears emerging down her cheeks. "No," she choked out and sped from the room. Word about Lloyd was getting around.

"Tammi, can you take over the sign-ups for now?" Anabel asked the concierge. This just might be one of the saddest Christmases yet in Hollywerth. I pulled out my phone and noted down the days and times of the events we planned to attend. Turning to talk to Mom, I spotted her back near the fireplace, animatedly talking to Maude. From my vantage point, those two looked like trouble waiting to happen.

CHAPTER FOUR

The odor of freshly brewed coffee permeated the air in the room as we started our day at Jules' coffee shop. Clinking glasses and the low rumble of early morning voices competed with the overhead speakers emitting upbeat Christmas music. Did the workers ever tire of hearing repeated songs, or did it just become background, white noise?

Mom was at the wall of pictures, pointing, "Chloe, look at this one." Past winners of the gingerbread house contest stood proudly next to their creations. Some of those looked like they had professional engineers designing them. Oh well, we would just be in it for the fun.

I placed our order and headed to a table. The cuteness of this place rivaled my friend Caroline's bakery back home in Cedarbrook. Though you couldn't go wrong with lots of Christmas-themed decorations to get people excited about the season and buying lots of goodies.

"Those houses look like experts designed them," Mom said, joining Max and me at the table.

"They're gorgeous." I gazed out the window as the snow drifted lazily to the ground. Our short walk to the coffee shop from the hotel chilled me, and I could really use the coffee to warm me up. I shivered and rubbed my arms, unable to get the vision of Lloyd out of my head. Anabel seemed genuinely surprised and upset at finding him, so it didn't appear that she could be a suspect. Unless she was an award-winning actress. Sherrie appeared the same when she got the news. Could the ousted Santa be at the top of the list? Was the competition for the coveted position that fierce in Hollywerth? Santa was a minor celebrity, and someone with an ego might just want revenge if they were replaced. But was that Lloyd's doing, or did someone else make that decision?

"Here you go, ladies," said the woman, approaching the table. "And who's this cutie?" She ruffled the fur on Max's head, causing it to stand up like Tina Turner's hair.

"That's Max. Our gingersnap-loving dog," I said.

Holding up a hand and scooting away from our table, the woman quickly returned with a small bag. Reaching past Max as he attempted to put his nose on it, she handed it to me. My little pooch was living large on this trip. Truthfully, he deserved that and more. He was a rescue, but really, he rescued me. After my husband passed, I didn't realize how lost I was until I met Max. He had become my partner in sleuthing. We only had a short amount of time before the family arrived and our time was spoken for. But, before then, we needed to carve a few minutes to puzzle this out.

"Thank you," I said, petting him. At this rate, we would both need to diet when we returned home. "I'm Chloe, by the way. This is my mom, Mabel." I waved my arm across the table.

"Welcome," the woman said. "I'm Jules. And this is my café. Glad you're here."

"It was kind of a rude welcome, though," Mom blurted. Not wrong, but I didn't want to gossip about something we knew little about.

Cuing in on Mom's point without saying the words, Jules' shoulders slumped, and she fiddled with a napkin on the table.

My eyes widened, and lips pursed, tilting my head at Mom. She was nothing if not direct. But time and place, Mom.

I sipped my coffee, trying to think of something to navigate away from the elephant in the room.

"We're looking forward to the gingerbread house contest. I only hope I can keep Max out of the ingredients," I said.

Max softly whimpered as Jules smiled, giving his right ear another brief scratch. "Yeah. It'll be tough going on with all the festivities without Lloyd this year." Jules gasped for a breath.

"Did you know him?" Mom quizzed. Her tone muted.

Nodding, Jules said, "We were dating and planning to get married."

"I'm so sorry," I said, with my brain about to explode. Was there trouble in paradise? What wasn't Jules saying? And was she truly broken up or putting on an act? What would her motive be? We needed to know more about Lloyd.

Max swiveled his head and stretched his neck in the direction of the café door. Several people entered, one of whom had a chocolate-colored lab. I placed my hand on Max's back, feeling his racing pulse. My normally chill guy appeared ready to pounce, though I wasn't sure to what end. I kept my hand on him until he retracted his neck and sat upright with a quick glance at me. As soon as my touch left him, he leapt from the chair in the dog's direction. Standing up, I bumped the table as the coffee swayed in the cups, threatening to lap over the edge. No way I could keep pace with Max to rein him in. He fast-walked right past the lab and the crowd and approached a product display carousel holding gift cards.

"Be right back," I said to Mom on my way to find out what Max was up to. He disappeared behind the card display and emerged with a small garden gnome in his mouth, proudly trotting over to me. I picked it up and looked for the display where he had found it. Facing the room, I scanned for other gnomes, finding none. It couldn't be. How did she manage that?

More closely scanning the gnome, I discovered a very familiar design. Flipping it over, I found the bottom of it labeled with Mom's business details. I had to hand it to her. I never would have thought of a marketing strategy where I left sample products around to be found like Easter eggs.

Max trotted alongside me, returning to our table, as he appeared proud as punch for his find. Who knew his hunting dog instincts would be on the prowl for garden gnomes?

Holding the gnome in front of me, I said, "Mom?" actually quite impressed with her marketing creativity.

"Chloe, you have to think outside the box," she replied. I secretly hoped I would be as spry when I reached my eighties, but I needed to temper my encouragement of her.

"Max outed you," I said, taking my seat. "But I have to hand it to you. That's quite the strategy to get your name out there beyond Cedarbrook."

"Maybe we could do some more trips that I could write off as a business expense if I sprinkle gnomes around the towns we go to."

"Maybe," I said. That would take us away from the treehouse for too long, unless we hired someone to manage while we were away. Actually, not a bad idea to consider bringing someone else on. Mom and I weren't getting any younger, and maybe we should plan some more fun times together.

"I have it. Now, Chloe, don't poo-poo my idea like you always do."

"Mom-" I stopped. Yes, that had become my default response. I was more conservative than she was and didn't always see the vision right away.

"How about a gnome museum in Cedarbrook?"

I sat, silently contemplating the concept but more thoroughly, my response. It wasn't a terrible idea. Guests at the treehouse had remarked how cute the little creatures were that Mom had placed throughout the grounds. There just might be something to that.

"Good idea, huh?" She took my lack of response as a maybe. Digging into her giant bag, she pulled out a small notepad and pen, furiously jotting down her thoughts.

"You might just have something," I said. If we went all in for gnomes at the treehouse, that unique touch just might be the most brilliant marketing move yet. Or not.

Max whimpered. Oh boy. Between him and Mom and those gnomes, this might just be an epic battle.

CHAPTER FIVE

Mom gasped as she clutched her bag on her lap, slightly tilting to her right. Oh no! My brain was practiced in going from zero to calamity in one second. I couldn't help myself. After growing up with the responsibility to care for my three siblings while my mostly single mom worked all the time, I had become accustomed to taking care of issues.

I reached across the table as Max sped to her side, his front paws on her thigh. "Mom. What is it?" I rose in my seat, scanning for some sign of a medical condition, ready to yell for someone to call 9-1-1.

"Chloe," she whispered loudly, flicking her head toward the door.

Did I miss a gnome? Were there more distributed throughout the café?

Leaning in, she held her hand to the side of her mouth. "Do you know who that is?" She lifted her right hand and pointed a finger toward a tall, good-looking man who had just entered the café.

Who would she recognize in Hollywerth, many hours away from home? The man was significantly younger, so he likely wasn't a former boyfriend. His salt-and-pepper, short hair put him about my age or a bit younger. He dressed in a light-blue, button-down shirt covered by a down vest, faded jeans topping cowboy boots.

Mom raised her arm, "Yoo hoo! Karl."

What was I missing that she even knew his name? Maybe he had been a guest at the hotel whom she had checked in when I wasn't there. I was sure I would have remembered him.

Karl returned the wave as the younger woman with him ushered him to the counter to order, narrowing her eyes at Mom. She must have been half his age, a May-December relationship. Karl leaned in to the woman and diverted his route to our table as the woman crossed her arms and tapped her foot.

"Do I know you?" Karl said, reaching to shake Mom's hand. Max returned to his seat, wiggling from side to side. Karl chuckled. "May I pet your dog?"

I smiled. "Of course. Thank you for asking."

"You should. I'm Mabel. A huge fan."

27

"Well, thank you for that," Karl said.

"Chloe, can you believe we're meeting a movie star?"

Mom always had her shows she watched and chatted about with the garden club. For me, my down time was a good book or puzzle with Max, quiet time with a huckleberry cocktail. "Nice to meet you. I'm Chloe, this is Max." My boy continued to fidget in his seat. Was he star-struck as well?

"Karl, we need to go," said his companion, reaching from behind to tug his elbow.

"Just a sec, Athena." Turning his attention to Mom, he continued, "If you have something you'd like me to autograph, I'd be happy to do that."

Mom plunged her arm into her purse, rummaging around. She stopped and grabbed the small gnome on the table, her eyes sparkling. "How about this?" she held it out to him.

"A gnome?" He looked at me and I nodded. "Nobody has ever asked me to autograph a gnome before." Karl withdrew a pen from his vest pocket, turning the gnome face down and writing on the back.

"Chloe, you really should watch the show. Karl is fabulous," Mom said. Turning her focus back to Karl, "I really like that Kelly character, too."

"What's it called?" I asked.

"Cameo Hills. About a ranching family trying to keep their land from big business," Mom piped up.

Karl grinned widely. "Maybe you should be on the marketing team for the production."

"Karl," Athena mumbled through gritted teeth.

"Athena's right. It's a good thing I have an assistant to keep me on schedule. I have an appearance later that I need to get prepared for."

"Oh, wait!" Mom shouted. "You should come to Cedarbrook and stay in one of our treehouses." She really was good at the promotion part of the business. Maybe I should give her free rein to do what she did best. She shined being the face of the business, where my skills were much better used behind the scenes for operations.

"That sounds like quite an adventure. Maybe I will," Karl said.

Athena rolled her head from side-to-side, sighing loud enough for us all to hear. She was just doing her job, but boy, did she have a poor attitude.

Mom squealed. I saw the wheels turning in her head about sharing this experience back home with the garden club. I wasn't sure they would even believe her. More than once she'd regaled them with an outlandish but true experience.

"You know. I have an idea," Karl said.

"This is getting ridiculous! I'm going to order," Athena said. Probably a good idea, as Mom seemed to have captivated Karl.

"We're filming nearby in Oakville after the holidays. We've got a scene in a restaurant in the town where we could use some extras," Karl looked between Mom and me.

"I'm going to be a movie star!" Mom yelled, drawing the attention of everyone in the café.

"Mabel. I can't promise that it's even a speaking part," Karl said.

Too late. I am sure Mom was already thinking about the dress she would buy to walk the red carpet.

"I have to find Maude. She would be great in there too," Mom said, inviting her new friend. "She's kind of like me, Karl. Very fashionable and up on all the latest things," Mom said to Karl. She just met Maude. How could she know that?

"OK," he replied. I suspected he might be regretting his invitation. No doubt Mom would take over the scene. I only hoped if she made it to the filming that they didn't cut her part. That would devastate her.

Max subtly slipped off his chair and stood next to Karl, leaning against his leg. How that little boy could communicate without words was impressive. I gestured for him to return to his seat. His gaze avoided my eye contact, stubbornly angling further away from me.

"Maybe Max wants a part too," Karl said, reaching to pat Max on his back.

No doubt if he was in a scene, he would steal it, just as he did everywhere he went.

"Karl, we're late. We really need to go now." Athena returned with a to-go tray holding coffee and pastries.

"Nice to meet you all. Athena will be in touch," Karl said, reaching for Mom's hand and gently kissing it. He turned with Athena behind him, as she glared at Mom with her eyes squinted almost shut.

"Well, he's dreamy. But she's quite the snotty girl," Mom said. She called it like she saw it and was hardly ever wrong.

"Yeah. He seems really nice. And what a generous offer for a scene in the show." Could we swing that? Oakville was even further away from home than Hollywerth. It was a once-in-a-lifetime opportunity for Mom. I would have to find a way to swing it. And to start watching Cameo Hills. I imagined Mom would want to chat about the show and apparently I had a few seasons to catch up on.

"This is turning out to be the best trip," Mom said. It warmed my heart to see her so happy.

"We should probably finish up here to get to Santa's workshop for the pictures." I looked at my watch, sure a line was already forming for the kiddos to visit Santa and share their wishes.

CHAPTER SIX

Max tugged the leash as we wound our way to the center of town to Santa's workshop. My boy was generally trustworthy to behave off-leash at home, but there were just too many distractions here. I couldn't wait to come out at night to see everything illuminated. Lights wrapped around every tree and lined every building. Christmas music piped from outside speakers. I tucked Mom's hand under my free arm to help her stabilize on the snowy sidewalks. The smell of baking pastry wafted through the air as we passed the Bavarian Kitchen. Slowing to peek into their window display case, I made a mental note of several things I wanted to sample.

Mom had a faraway look on her face and was unusually quiet. The encounter with Karl must still be on her mind. I still couldn't figure out how those kinds of things always seemed to happen to her.

She kept herself open to adventure, and that vibe attracted a lot of enjoyment.

"This is magical," she said.

I couldn't agree more. In a short amount of time, I decided I wanted to return, sure that we wouldn't have time to take in everything we planned. Turning toward the gazebo in the center of the park, Max again tugged the leash, this time toward Santa. He had seen people in costume before, but I couldn't predict how he would react. The line to see Santa had indeed grown. Mom and I navigated to the end to wait our turn. Kids bounced around, sharing with their parents what they would request from Santa. To our left was a small hill where several families had sledding discs and were traversing up and down the smooth snow. What a brilliant strategy to tire out the little tykes.

Several of Santa's elves worked the line from both sides, entertaining the waiting group with simple tricks and jokes. Max sat on his haunches, the perfect audience. I stepped close enough that my leg touched him. He leaned into me.

As we moved forward in the line, the elves from our left got closer, one leaning into the other, and not so quietly saying, "I think that dad did it. You remember how furious he was when his kid left Santa?" The second elf bobbed his head, his droopy cap dangling from side-to-side.

Gossip in front of the crowd waiting for Santa seemed unprofessional. But did I just glean another clue in this puzzle? Could a parent be so enraged about something Santa said to his kid that he would take action? These days some parents became judge, jury, and executioner if their kid was put out in the slightest.

"Yeah, Lloyd was a tell it like it was kind of person. When the kid asked for a unicorn, Lloyd laughed his head off, telling the kid to get real," the second elf said. "Who do we have here?" The elf crouched and grasped each of Max's ears for a nice scratch. Max closed his eyes, taking in the attention.

"This is Max. I'm Chloe, and this is my mom, Mabel," I said. How could I interrogate them without being too obvious?

"Welcome to Hollywerth," said the first elf. "I hope you enjoy your stay."

They both stepped past us to continue working the line. "Is that a new Santa?" I asked.

In unison, their heads pivoted toward each other. They didn't know that I knew, and I hoped to use that to my advantage.

"Chloe, you know—" Mom started.

I quickly glared at her to stop talking. She got the message and took a small step backward, allowing my inquisition to continue.

"Yes. Well, not new," said the first elf. He moved closer to me, glancing around to check who was within earshot. "Greg was the Santa before Lloyd."

Waiting for more, they rewarded me for my patience.

"It was quite the competition when Lloyd was selected over Greg, who had been the Santa for over ten years. He was like a minor celebrity in town." Was the coveted Santa position so prestigious that Greg would take Lloyd out to return to his seat of glory?

"Steven," said the first elf. "We should keep moving." She furrowed her brows. Not a good look for the elves to be dissing Santa, especially a dead one.

As they prepared to move on, I attempted one more question. "Who decided to replace Greg?"

The first elf grabbed Steven's elbow and led him further from us. "Oh, it was Anabel." Steven said over his shoulder as he was roundly escorted away.

A vision of a puzzle outline formed in my head. In a short amount of time, three suspects emerged in the death of Lloyd. From the group, who had the strongest motive? An angry father? A dethroned Santa? But if Anabel had chosen Lloyd, was there something going on behind the scenes with those two? One more kid in line before our turn to see

Santa. I prepared my questions for the brief opportunity I would have with Greg to elicit any further clues.

Our turn was up. Santa patted the chair next to him that was angled in about ninety degrees. Max hopped up like a pro, half-way facing Santa and looking toward the camera. Santa placed his hand on Max's back as the photographer snapped several photos.

"You got yourself a dutiful pup there," Santa said, his belly bouncing.

"He's more behaved than many people I know," I said.

"Yeah. I get that," Santa said. "Thanks for stopping by." He dismissed us.

"This is our first time in Hollywerth. You seem like a pro at this," I smiled, hoping to prompt an opening for a follow-up question.

"I feel like I was born to do this. Love chatting up the little ones and seeing the sparkle in their eyes as they share their wishes for what they hope to see under the tree Christmas morning." He waved up the next in line to join him, our chat coming to a close.

"I understand there was supposed to be a new Santa this year," I said, taking every second to squeeze what I could from him.

Santa dipped his head. His jowls sagged.

Patting my leg, I gestured for Max to leave the chair for the child to be seated.

Santa scooted the chair about an inch closer to him and fidgeted in his seat. Clearly, I was being dismissed.

"Thank you again," I said, hoping to thaw the ice that had formed around him.

"I will post your photos on-line in a few hours at the hotel website under your room number," the photographer said.

Mom, Max, and I moved to the side of Santa's workshop. My heart pounded through the layers of clothes. Greg did not appear to be one you toyed with. From that interaction, he flew to the top of my suspect list. To be ousted as Santa after all those years must have been embarrassing for him. What lengths would he go to in order to return to the sought-after role?

"Chloe, on the way back to our room, let's go by the tree lighting place to stake out our position," Mom said.

"Mmm hmmm," I mumbled, shuddering. And not from the cold.

CHAPTER SEVEN

Max pranced as we left Santa's place. About twenty yards out, I stopped mid-stride, unable to shake my uneasiness from the encounter with Greg. Turning back, I watched him chuckling and engaging in lively conversations with the kids. He really seemed to be good at the job. Could I tease out from Anabel why Lloyd had replaced him without sending her off the deep end from a touchy subject? Tugging at the leash, Max attempted to get after some kids sledding down the small hill to our right. Maybe another time, buddy. The pure joy displayed on their faces wrapped in hoods, showing only eyeballs and rosy cheeks and noses, warmed my heart. Was I too old to do something like that? And with a dog on my lap? Maybe I could just let Max loose for one run down the hill on his own. For now, I wanted to warm up.

Mom and I continued along the sidewalk, heading toward the Douglas fir tree towering in the center of the village. I imagined the lighting ceremony would be well-attended and quite the production, as was everything we had so far experienced in Hollywerth. We stopped just short of the tree as Mom took a gander around. Max and I patiently waited for her decision to choose just the perfect viewing location. She took off toward some shops and pivoted in front of Snowshoe Brewing Company. "This is it," she said, looking one hundred eighty degrees from left to right. There was a small podium near the tree on this side of the street, where I assumed the emcee would stand, leading the ceremony.

"This looks great. It's supposed to start at 6 p.m. so we'll need to decide how long we want to stand in the cold to save our spot," I said. I would be satisfied with several rows back from the front. There wouldn't be a bad spot to view the lighting. After all, the tree appeared to be at least one hundred feet tall.

"Well, Chloe," Mom thumbed her hand behind us. "We could always start with an adult beverage."

"A cold beer?"

"Why not?"

Indeed, why not? That woman continued to stretch me from my comfort zone. And it hadn't ended up in too much of a disaster yet.

Returning to Cedarbrook to help Mom with the treehouse hotel had provided us the opportunity to repair our relationship. After leaving town when I graduated high school, there weren't many return trips to visit her or my siblings. I was torn with some regret at missing so much, no matter my feelings about our childhood. My self-centered view lost me years with my mom. Maybe the distance provided me some perspective on the challenges she had as a mostly single mom raising four kids, some of whom were rebels. My role as the most responsible to step in with supervision when she was gone had trained me to be a leader in my professional life. My goal for our remaining time together was to live our life to the fullest.

"I signed us up for a sleigh ride after dinner. I figured we may want to do that before the crowds swarm," I said.

Max jerked the slack leash from my hand as he raced toward the Christmas tree. I squinted in his direction, pursuing him. "Max!" I didn't see a critter or any suspect that would cause him to bolt. "Max!"

He had a one-track mind as he ignored me. Was he just going to pee on it? At home, there was an abundance of trees on many of our walks that provided ample options for relieving himself. Did his sense of smell catch a scent of something hidden to my eyes? Mom chuckled behind me, as I'm sure the sight was quite humorous. Slowing to a trot, he disappeared behind the trunk. I circled the tree, lifting the snow-weighted branches, thoroughly dusting myself. Another round of laughter from Mom. Coming around to my right, proud as punch, Max had a garden gnome in his mouth. The bright red cap portion of the creature stuck out of his mouth. He dropped it at my feet and sat.

I didn't even have to look further to know that it was one from Mom's collection. How in the world did she get around to hide these? Did she sneak out at night? Or have an accomplice? Some of her secrets I would probably never know. Or want to find out. Tucking the gnome into my pocket, I grabbed the leash and returned to Mom.

She shook her head, grinning from ear-to-ear. So far it was Max three, Mom zero, but I suspected the game was far from over. The layers of snow covering the ground muted most sounds. The joyous music and laughing visitors filled the air.

We headed back to the hotel to get ready for dinner. Moving past the sliding doors into the lobby, warm air blasted my face. Thankfully, we weren't leaving the grounds again to reach the restaurant. I loved the beauty of the snow, but I had my limits.

"I'm looking forward to dinner," Mom said. I had reluctantly agreed to the German place to eat, hoping her stomach could take the spicy, rich food. Or more accurately, my gut.

We followed her through the lobby to the hallway with the elevators, passing the Nutcracker museum. She stopped at the same place we were yesterday when all heck broke loose. The door was closed, likely allowing for an investigation to proceed. "Mom," I said.

"It's so sad, Chloe." Yes, it was. Saying goodbye to a loved one at any time was difficult, but the circumstances of a murder complicated the situation exponentially. "Oh, look." Mom stepped to the door and opened it for the police officer to exit.

"I'm sorry, ladies, it's still closed for now," he said, stepping into the hallway. From the hardware on his uniform, I figured he was a ranking officer.

"Of course," Mom said.

"Do you have any idea who could have done it, officer?" I asked, Greg's comments at the forefront of my mind.

"You—" the officer started.

Nodding, I said, "Yes. We were here when Anabel found him."

Looking left and right, he lowered his voice. "Call me Thomas. We're still working to figure that out." Yep, tight-lipped. Should I share what I knew? Was it really anything more than speculation or gossip? Not wanting to convolute the investigation, I pursed my lips as Mom entered the shop.

"Ma'am," Thomas said, watching her escape from sight. Little did he know she would not be deterred.

"I'm sure she'll be right out," I said. By now I had caught onto her mission. If you can't beat 'em, join 'em.

Certain he would look at Greg as a suspect, I offered a couple of other angles. "I wonder if it was a disgruntled parent. Or even an elf."

Glancing over his shoulder as Mom exited the museum, he said, "Possible."

"Officer," Mom held out her hand. "Thank you for keeping us safe."

Thomas glanced at me as I shrugged.

CHAPTER EIGHT

I held my stomach, feeling it rumble with the bratwurst and sauerkraut combination churning up some gas. The server had recommended the combo as a favorite of guests. I wanted to do it at least once to soak in the Bavarian experience. My gut was telling me to stick to something more neutral. Mom had pep in her step right beside me as we made our way to the sleigh ride station. If she was feeling the effects of dinner, I couldn't tell. Or maybe it was just propelling her along. We were as bundled as you could get for the cold evening. Hats, scarves, gloves, hand warmers in our pockets, fur-lined boots. My little guy sported a Christmas sweater and a Santa hat, prancing along at Mom's pace. It was a challenge to keep up with them, but I was grateful for the movement.

Holding my stomach, I groaned.

"Chloe, I told you not to eat so much of that."

"I know. But it was so good." How was she not keeled over with what she ate?

The sky had cleared, with stars showing faintly overhead, their sparkle drowned out by the village's light show. Almost every surface in the entire town twinkled, showing so much light that it appeared as daytime.

Passing by the gazebo, Santa's workshop was closed for the night, a sign showing a very early morning opening. The person holding that position had the center of attention during the holiday season, and likely throughout the year as well. Was Greg's ego so large that he would do harm to Lloyd in order to keep the position? Was Greg shamed by the loss of the role of a lifetime?

"Chloe, look." Mom abruptly stopped, pointing to an ice-skating rink in the distance, young and old sliding their way around the circle.

"No way," I said. That's all I needed, something broken.

"But it's so romantic. You and Paul should do it when he arrives," Mom said, taking off again.

My boyfriend would be here soon, joining our crazy family on this winter adventure. How he stuck around after getting to know us was beyond me. And going into business with my mom for her gnome production blew my mind. He really seemed to get her, even more than her own kids did. The two of them together in Mom's garage workshop were quite adorable. Paul allowed Mom to boss him around, and that was probably a key ingredient that made the relationship work. How did I get so lucky to find love a second time in my life?

Max leaped ahead as we neared the corral with the reindeer and the sleigh ride location. He didn't get to see too many animals larger than him at home and mostly chased the squirrels and rabbits. It was a game he loved, and I imagined he thought they did as well. When he finished his pursuits around the treehouse grounds, he would return to the office, tongue lolling to the side of his mouth, grinning from ear to ear and completely spent.

I gently pulled the leash toward me as Max strained away. They decorated the fence containing the animals with lights and evergreen boughs. The reindeer sported red and green scarves with bells dangling under their chins, quietly jingling every time they shook their heads. A familiar face was standing near the sleigh, chatting with the woman who was hooking up the reins. Their heads bowed together, speaking in hushed tones. The woman worked her way around all four reindeer, lashing them to the sleigh. Not sure what to expect, I hoped for a leisurely ride around the grounds to give us an opportunity to see sights we hadn't yet visited.

We stopped just outside the gate, waiting for permission to enter. "Hello," Mom offered in a sing-songy voice.

Sherrie turned around and raised her hand. "Hello, everyone. Glad you could join us." She unhooked the two latches on the gate and open it for us to enter. Glancing over her shoulder, she asked, "Melody? Just about ready?"

Max sat near me, his excitement tempered as the reindeer towered over him.

Melody said, "Just about. One more to go." She tugged firmly on one of the buckles, prompting the reindeer to stumble.

"How fast do you go?" Mom asked. Knowing her, she was ready for a sprint. No doubt if we were at an amusement park she would beeline to the roller coaster, not slowing down at all for her age. If anything, she seemed to get more adventurous.

Laughing, Sherrie said, "It's basically a fast walk."

Melody finished the prep and said, "Ready to roll." She came around and extended her hand to Mom to step up into the sleigh. It was also lined with evergreen trim, lights, and red felt bows.

Mom scooted to the far seat behind the driver as Max and I followed suit, my boy seated between us, on high alert for the next action.

"Let me just switch that on," Sherrie said, reaching toward the floor of the sleigh where a small heater was located. Now this was my kind of ride. "Everyone ready?" she asked.

"Onward." Mom raised her arm. Melody opened the gate at the end of the corral, and we began our tour.

I wrapped my arm around Max, feeling him slightly shaking. Moving close enough for our bodies to touch, I leaned in. He quickly glanced at me, then shifted his focus to the front. Was he a little frightened? Or was he just cold? Or maybe the shaking was excitement at this new experience?

Sherrie bent over and withdrew three small bags of gingersnaps, handing them back to us. No matter what might bother Max, having his favorite treat would certainly settle him down. He stood, wiggling from side to side, bumping both Mom and me.

"Glad to see you ladies again," Sherrie said, steering us to the right along a path into the trees. "Are you enjoying your time in Hollywerth?"

"Well, you know, except for finding Santa dead," Mom said.

Whipping my head to the right, I pursed my lips and glared.

"It's true," Mom said, furrowing her brows at me.

Sherrie flicked the reins, inciting the reindeer to gear up a notch. Max bounced on the seat next to me as the ride got bumpier.

Hoping to settle things down, I asked, "Did you know Lloyd well?"

After a significantly delayed response while she drove us through the trees, Sherrie replied, "Yes." She wiped her glove across her face.

"I'm sorry for your loss," I said.

"That woman worked him to the bone," Sherrie continued. "I felt sorry for him." Was she referring to Anabel? From our brief encounter at the museum, it was tough to judge her personality.

Emerging from the forest, Sherrie navigated us along a street that appeared to be blocked off for the sole purpose of a sleigh ride, not slowing down one bit.

Had there been a confrontation between boss and employee that got out of hand?

"She was so overbearing, I couldn't understand why he stayed with her," Sherrie said, confirming my suspicion of a possible romantic relationship between Anabel and Lloyd, further complicating the picture of suspects.

Another trip to the museum was in order to investigate Anabel.

Sherrie slowed us down as we returned to the corral.

"Chloe, you and Paul have to do this. It's so romantic," Mom said. From the get go, she had been a matchmaker between the two of us, at first against my wishes. But she didn't give up, thankfully, seeing the potential of mine and Paul's relationship. I owed her a lot for that.

We exited the sleigh, reversing our directions to return to the hotel. "I think we should check out that nutcracker museum again," I said.

Mom squealed. "I knew you'd come around to the idea of a gnome museum."

Missing my intent, I realized I should have more carefully chosen my words. Since Paul was encouraging her gnome business, maybe I could enlist him for this venture. But first things first. I needed another meeting with Anabel. Could she have killed Lloyd? All the factors were there.

CHAPTER NINE

The quiet of the early morning lobby filled with the crackles from the fire, and the softly playing Christmas music from the overhead speakers. In the two days since we had arrived in Hollywerth, I had rarely heard songs repeated. Genres played spanned from classic religious melodies to rockin' jazz. The crowds would significantly pick up the closer we got to Christmas.

Sipping my coffee, I jotted down notes for our restaurant opening plans. The family in Cedarbrook that had owned Merano's had closed down after the owner had been murdered. The location and facility were perfectly suited for our family's vision. The romanticized version of this venture allured the Carson clan to band together. Was this a disaster waiting to happen? Mom was aging, but not in the least slowing down. Was she really up to the partnership, and were her kids up to it? She was a different woman from when we grew up. We had all changed, and time had forgiven much of the hurt. In her shoes, I truthfully don't think I could have done any better. And, really, all of us were happy, healthy, productive members of society.

I pulled my boy closer, giving him a squeeze. He gazed up at me with large, warm brown eyes, radiating love. Finishing my restaurant idea brainstorm, I turned the page in my notebook to jot down thoughts on clues for Lloyd's murder. My head spun with so many suspects that I needed to create some order out of the chaos.

Max placed his front paws on my thighs and poked his snout toward the page. He and I had become quite a puzzling team. Back home in our treehouse, the favorite evening activity was a puzzle, a huckleberry cocktail for me, and gingersnaps for Max. Together, we attempted to solve the problems of the world. We started with number types of puzzles, soduko and kenken. Those were easy enough for Max to take part in by tapping his paw to show a number. He even won a bingo round at a fund-raiser for senior high school scholarships. The day I challenged him by pulling out a crossword puzzle, I could tell his feelings were hurt. His jowls sagged as he tipped his head toward me, his bushy eyebrows poking together. However, it wasn't long before we had a system where he easily solved those. Today, a new one for him I was sure he would like.

On a blank page, I drew a grid. Down the left side, I listed all the names of suspects. Along the top, I labeled three columns: Motive, Means, Opportunity. Tilting the page toward Max, he grinned. Now for the names. Anabel, since she discovered the body. Greg. Jules. The angry elf, Steven. Sherrie. The disgruntled parent. Wow! Just looking at the list on paper, I wondered, did anyone like Lloyd? How in the world did he displace the previous Santa who had held the role for such a long time if he was that disliked? Did he have leverage over the decision makers? And who were they? With my schedule about to get very busy when family arrived, there was little time to investigate.

I pointed to the first name on the list and settled my pencil in the first column. Max tipped his head. I too was unsure of a motive for Anabel. Maybe more would come out later. Moving my pencil to the second column, I drew an X. Max nodded. Same for column three. That was easy, two out of three for Anabel.

Next up, Greg. What did we know about him? His motive topped the list. Max tapped the paper, confirming the X I wrote in that square. The only question was: how would Greg have entered and exited the museum since the front door was locked? Did he have a key for some reason? And was there another entrance? It was an easy conclusion: he would be the prime suspect. But things aren't always as they seem.

Mom's voice boomed from across the lobby. Her laughter filled the festive air. It warmed my heart that she was thoroughly enjoying herself. Max and I looked her direction to see giggles like two schoolgirls between her and Maude.

"Oh, Chloe," Mom said, collapsing into the overstuffed chair on the opposite side of the space from Max and I. Maude settled into the chair next to her. My spidey sense elevated to maximum level, wondering what high jinks the two of them had gotten into. Mom by herself was typically suspected of some shenanigans, but with Maude as her partner, the odds of trouble skyrocketed. "Who knew video games could be so much fun?"

I waited for more explanation from my increasingly eclectic mother.

"Mabel is a natural. I let her take over my controller for a while," Maude chimed in. "She wiped the floor with that kid."

"Maude invited me to go with her to the gamer tournament." Mom clapped her hands. "The only thing is I need to come up with a gamer name."

Not sure what I was seeing right in front of my eyes, I asked, "What kind of game?"

"It's football," Maude said. "We play a season, drafting players and everything."

Looking at Mom, I could see her gears spinning at top speed. She tapped her finger on her chin, then raised her arm in victory. "I've got it!"

Draping my arm over Max, we braced for her next sentence.

"So Maude's gamer name is Slaya65. I think mine should be Gnomie65. Get it?"

Nodding, I said, "Cute." Was she just going along with Maude, or did she really enjoy video games? I wasn't seeing it, but I had learned to expect the unexpected from her. To date, she hadn't had much interest in sports. She proved repeatedly it was never too late for new life experiences.

"We should make plans to meet up again later," Maude said.

Was this distraction going to divert our family's plans for the reunion and business venture? I was all for Mom enjoying herself, but we also had a job to do on this trip.

"What have you got there?" Mom asked, pointing to my notebook.

Tipping my head, I scanned the sparsely populated diagram, nothing apparent jumped out at me. "Well, we started with notes for the business. So when the rest of the family arrives, we could hit the ground running."

Mom turned toward Maude. "It was my idea to do a family business. And have all of my kids back together." She scooted to the edge of her seat, leaning toward me.

"I think you'll be pleased," I said. Despite her challenges in running the treehouse hotel, Mom was great at ideas and strategy. She really had a long-term vision. Thankfully, my skills came in handy with the execution and implementation. Many times, it took a lot of convincing for me to see the beauty of her dreams.

"Maude, look who's coming," Mom said, tilting her head over my left shoulder. Both women bolted up, grinning widely. I suspected there was only one person I had seen at the resort that would engender that type of response.

CHAPTER TEN

Maude giggled. Max hopped from his perch and sat tall, his bottom scooting from side to side with his wiggles. Turning to my left, I saw the tall, handsome Karl approach the seating area.

"Hello, everyone," he bent and grabbed Max's ears with both hands and gently rubbed. Max closed his eyes and leaned into it, almost toppling to the floor. I guess even dogs can swoon with a famous person in their midst.

"Where's that girl?" Maude quizzed him.

Karl stood, and Max bolted toward a Christmas tree in the lobby's corner. Several wrapped boxes were spread out at the base. I kept him in my peripheral vision to make sure he wasn't up to any mischief.

Karl chuckled. "Athena had some errands to run."

"She doesn't seem very nice," Maude continued.

"Yeah. She can be abrasive. Though she does have my best interest at heart," he said.

Mom groaned. "I wonder."

"Do you have family coming to meet you?" Maude quizzed him.

Karl might regret getting involved with these two chatty Cathys.

"Here, come sit," Mom said, returning to her seat and patting the chair next to her.

"Just for a minute." Karl followed the orders. "I've got a meeting with one of the Cameo Hills show producers in a bit."

"Oooooh," Maude said. She took the chair flanking Karl. He was now penned in by the seniors.

From the corner of my eye, a buff-colored streak emerged on my left side and stopped in the middle of the seating area. Another gnome, deposited for all to see. I think we were now up to four that Max had uncovered. How many more were there?

"What in the world?" Karl reached from his chair, picking up the slobbery creature with his thumb and pointer finger. He rotated it, lifting the bottom up to read the writing. "Mabel?" He held the little guy in Mom's direction.

"Why yes, Karl. That's one of mine. Just another of my businesses back home. We're going to open a gnome museum when we get back. Right, Chloe?"

Karl's eyebrows shot up, a smirk emerging on his lips, pieces of the Mabel puzzle continuing to fall into place for him. He retrieved a handkerchief from his pocket, setting the gnome on the side table and wiping the Max drool from his hands.

Max sauntered to Karl, leaning into his leg, looking for praise. "And this little guy. How did he know?" Karl asked.

"You have no idea," I said. "That's the fourth one he has found since we've arrived."

Karl tapped his temple with his finger and nodded to Mom.

"Yes, I know," she replied. "Genius."

"Perhaps Max is auditioning for a role in my show as well," Karl said, prompting Max to leap into Karl's lap and lick his face. No doubt my boy would shine in something like that. But where wasn't he a star?

"That's generous of you, but maybe another time," I said. If Mom ended up in the show somehow, that would be enough diva to handle. "Max."

Max snuggled closer to Karl. I shook my head, and he slid off the chair, slinking over to me and flopping hard onto the cushion.

"You like puzzles?" Karl asked, waving his hand toward my notebook.

"Yeah, that's one I made up myself." Looking down at the meager list of clues, I was skeptical they would solve the murder before our trip ended. With crowds of people descending on Hollywerth, I suspected the police had their hands full with normal holiday drama. And being such a small town, they would likely bring in reinforcements from other jurisdictions.

"Chloe is a brilliant detective. She'll solve Santa's murder in no time," Mom piped up.

"May I?" Karl reached for my notebook.

I reluctantly handed it over, concerned that I might have something wrong and send this investigation down the wrong path.

He bowed his head and rested his forearms on his knees, studying my handiwork.

Mom shrugged her shoulders as we all sat silently, waiting for his response.

"You've got quite a list there," Karl said. He sat back in the chair and crossed his legs, glancing back at the paper. "What does your gut tell you?"

Max barked. Did my boy know something that I didn't? Our diagram was hardly finished, but as usual, he was several steps ahead of me. He stood and barked again. The entire crowd in the lobby now watched us.

Karl returned the notebook. "I'm not sure I should say. I wouldn't want to wrongly accuse someone. That kind of rumor is something a person would never recover from." Truth be told, Greg was my top suspect. Though I tried to let the clues lead me to a conclusion.

"Yeah. You're right," Karl said. "Wouldn't want to be the one investigating this. No matter what happens, it's going to be spectacular. Someone killed Santa. That's big news no matter where you live."

He was right. That truth was stranger than the fiction world Karl worked in. Hollywerth probably didn't want that publicity. Likely, the murder of Santa in a Christmas-themed town was all over the news. Although a killer was still on the loose, there were people that kind of story would attract to this place.

"Karl," Maude said. "Tell us how it is to be a celebrity."

Chuckling, he shook his head. "Well, there certainly are perks."

"Ooooh, like what?" Maude continued. She folder her hands under her chin and perched her elbows on the arm of the chair. Her eyes sparkled. Granted, he was good looking and kind. And these seniors were smitten.

"Certainly the money can buy a lot of enjoyment and make life quite easy. And I can donate to a lot of causes that I'm passionate about," Karl said, humoring his small but engaged audience.

"Do you know Anne Dawson?" Mom asked. I had no idea who that was or how she knew the name since she rarely watched TV and never went to the movies.

"I do. She's very nice. We were in a movie together several years ago that I also directed," Karl continued.

"Ahhh," Maude groaned, closing her eyes.

Whether or not he knew it, he was giving these ladies an experience of a lifetime. I was sure it would live on in Mom's stories to her garden club. I had a whole new respect for Karl, knowing he didn't have to give them the time of day.

"What causes are you involved in?" I asked.

"Thank you for asking. One that I'm very passionate about is rescuing horses. We have a lot of them on the set of Cameo Hills, and it's become very important to me they are treated well."

Anyone who had that level of care for animals was OK in my book.

"I should probably go, or Athena will have my hide," Karl said. He stood and turned toward Mom and Mabel. "Ladies, it's been an absolute delight." Leaving the area, Karl winked at me. Even if that was an award-winning performance, he left those two ladies riding a high.

Maude leaned half-way out of her chair, her gaze followed Karl's behind.

CHAPTER ELEVEN

Mom had been in a daze since our meeting earlier today with Karl. She had napped for a few hours, and I was grateful she had taken a break. We had a lot on our plate for the upcoming days and a bit of a late night as we headed to the tree lighting ceremony. Snow had drifted down on and off all day. I hoped we would have a break during the lighting, mostly for our safety walking to the location we had scouted out. How did I let Mom talk me into eating at another gut-bomb restaurant? I would have to find the most mild dish on the Bacon and Brews menu. Was eating spicy food part of her success in living a long life? I couldn't see how. Every time I did it, I was certain I lost several hours of my life.

Looping her arm through mine, we exited the elevator. The constant Christmas tunes flowed through overhead speakers into every room. "Silent Night" lyrics soothed us as we passed the door to the nutcracker museum. Lights blazed inside, illuminating the displays along the walls as guests milled around, appearing unaware of the murder that had occurred there a few days prior. I visualized the chart Max and I had prepared. All indications circled back to Greg. He was the obvious choice from the motive perspective. However, Anabel topped the list for the opportunity and means. I still couldn't wrap my brain around a motive for her, since she had hired Lloyd.

Sighing, I resigned myself to the fact we may not have a conclusion to the mystery before we left town. Max trotted to my left, the leash slack. Normally he obeyed my commands to stay close, but too many temptations appeared at every turn for that to be successful in Hollywerth.

"Chloe, I am so happy," Mom said.

We navigated along the sidewalk through the growing crowd. Families with giggling children, shoppers with arms full of bags, couples strolling with hands held. Disneyland held nothing over Hollywerth for the happiest place on earth.

Turning into Bacon and Brews, the warmth of the room blanketed my body. I shivered to shake off the chill. Most every table was filled, and the buzz of the chatter overtook the Christmas music.

I stepped to the hostess stand and gave her our names from the reservation. She grabbed a couple of menus, bent to pat Max, and led us to our table near a window. We had a perfect view of what would soon be the Christmas tree lighting ceremony, but I was certain Mom would want to be outside for that. It's not that I didn't like to be outdoors. Cedarbrook and the treehouse hotel were located in quite a bit of nature. Max and I regularly ventured out to many locations and enjoyed getting away. If I had my preference, I would always choose warmer weather.

"What should I have? There are so many choices," Mom said, running her finger down the list of menu items.

Looking for the mildest option I could find, it seemed like a BLT was going to be it. That shouldn't be too bad for my stomach.

"Ooooh, I see it. Bacon chili nachos." Mom folded her menu and slid it to the edge of the table. "I see several dishes that could inspire the menu at our restaurant."

The server arrived and took our drink and food order. We each ordered a variation of the local Icicle Brewing Company beer. I was certain my brother, the chef, would develop some locally inspired creations for our restaurant in Cedarbrook. Truthfully, I was more excited than anything about this collaboration. I kept the negative thoughts and concerns at bay by asking myself, *What if everything goes well?* We had all the right ingredients for success, and I focused on the potential.

"What should we do when your sisters arrive tomorrow?" Mom asked. Zoe, Joey, and I were triplets. How mom ever raised four kids, mostly on her own, boggled my mind. Heaven knows, a couple of us didn't make it easy on her. That woman exemplified grit, and for that I was grateful that I had inherited a smidgen of it.

"We haven't really done any shopping yet," I said. The shops here were pricey, but I owed it to myself to scout them out for any treasures and souvenirs. I didn't know if we would ever return to Hollywerth. We had just begun our time, and the drama and excitement were off the charts.

"Mmmm," Mom mumbled, gazing out the window.

"Good riddance is all I can say," came a booming voice from across the room. I slightly shifted my head in the direction of the outburst to see Greg sitting with Jules.

Mom leaned in, quickly catching a glance of the two. "What do you think that's about?"

"I assume he's not heartbroken by Lloyd's death," I said. With the current Santa out of the way, it made room for Greg to return, at least until another replacement could be secured. But at this late date, he probably had the position, at least temporarily.

"Can't you at least have some sympathy?" Jules said, sniffling. "I loved him."

Greg's voice softened, "Sis, I know you did. But I will not fake despair over a guy that didn't deserve you. Or anyone, for that matter."

"Chloe," Mom whispered, her hand cupping the left side of her mouth.

I scrambled to open my purse, retrieving my small notebook. Max stood and stepped out from under the table. I held out my hand to ease his mind about any trouble. He looked at Mom and returned to his spot near my feet.

Greg shook his head. "I wish you hadn't fallen for him. That guy could BS with the best of 'em."

"I know you didn't like him because he got the Santa position."

Holding out his hand, Greg said, "That's not it. Of course, I think the hiring decision was wrong, but he was just not a good dude."

"He promised me he was leaving Anabel. And I know he was telling the truth."

Jotting down notes, I starred Greg's name, feeling even more confident in his potential guilt. His motive got stronger with this new revelation of his sister's involvement with a guy he despised. Was it enough for him to kill Lloyd? Could he and Lloyd have been arguing about his involvement with Jules and it got out of hand? Or was he just an overprotective brother?

The server brought our beer and said the food would be out shortly. I sipped the foamy beverage tinged with a hint of cinnamon. Not really a beer person, but this might change my mind. And the alcohol would certainly soothe my nerves. In reality, a killer still walked among us. Was he sitting right across the room?

I gazed outside at the hustle of the crew prepping for the lighting ceremony. They placed a podium with a microphone to one side of the tree. Small crowds had formed, early birds taking their perch for the best view. I glanced back at Jules and Greg, their heads bowed toward each other, as the server arrived with our food.

CHAPTER TWELVE

T he BLT and the beer so far had settled well on my stomach. But my brain twisted around the conversation we overheard from Jules and Greg. Taking each of them separately through my questions, I still couldn't attach them to all the clues. Each person on my list had a reason to take down Lloyd. All had the means with the nutcracker used to bash him over the head. The opportunity question was the biggest hole in my theories. Except for the obvious Anabel who discovered the body, how could any of the others have made it into the museum without detection?

Mom and I scooted out of the booth to head toward our chosen viewing location for the tree lighting. Jules and Greg were long gone. As we exited the restaurant, the slight breeze blew snowflakes through the open door. I tightened the scarf around my neck and drew out my earmuffs.

Donning her neon green stocking cap, Mom turned and said, "I'll be right back. I forgot something."

Sure, Mom. Max whimpered, craning his neck toward me. We had her number by this time. Her bag bulged from what I could only guess were more gnomes that she planned to leave around town. On the positive side, her bag would be much lighter for the trip home. And who knew? Maybe getting her name out into the world would come back to her in ways she couldn't even imagine. And if she enjoyed what she was doing, who was I to argue?

"OK. I'll meet you at the spot we picked out. Don't be too long," I said.

Raising her arm as she scurried away, I heard, "I won't." At the end of the sidewalk, Maude joined up with Mom, the two of them arm-in-arm. Oh boy. Now the chance of shenanigans rose exponentially. Was that a happenstance meeting or had they planned something?

Max and I ambled along the sidewalk, taking in all the sights. The setup for the tree lighting was complete. I expected the event to be nothing short of spectacular, like all the other activities in town, done to the hilt.

"It won't be long now," the announcer blared over the loudspeaker. The volume of the music raised, in line with the level of excitement about illuminating the tree. I shoved my sleeve back to reveal the time on my watch, looking around for Mom. How far had she gone? The crowds thickened, which would make it more of a challenge for her to return to me. Thankfully, we had picked out a location ahead of time. Oh well. If she watched the ceremony from a different spot, so be it. Max and I parked in a little cubby hole of people at the edge of the sidewalk.

"Hi, Chloe," Anabel said, joining me from across the street. She rubbed her arms like she was trying to warm up.

I looked at the cloudy night sky, the lights from the town glowing so much it felt like twilight instead of evening.

Anabel bent to greet Max with a pat. My boy stepped toward me, bumping my leg. Was he avoiding Anabel? The sidewalk filled in quickly as people took up their positions. Glancing around to see if Mom's hat was bobbing toward me, I couldn't spot her anywhere. Though her small stature could have been swallowed up by the throng.

"Where's Mabel? Is she OK?" Anabel asked, standing to face me.

"Yes. She had a quick errand to run. But she should be here any moment." At times, I worried about my eighty-year-old, frail mother. But she was a tough old bird, able to hold her own.

I heard, "Excuse me. Pardon me" as I saw her elbowing a path to reach me. Maude was nowhere in sight. Sure enough, Mom's big bag looked deflated.

Shaking my head, I held out my hand to pull her through the last steps to reach us.

"Whew, that was close," Mom said, wiping her brow with her matching neon green, gloved hand.

Did she mean she almost didn't make the ceremony? Or did she escape detection in her escapades? I waited for more detail, but none was forthcoming. Would I ever know where she had gone off to? I draped my arm around her and pulled her closer to my side.

"Hi, Mabel," Anabel said, leaning around me to greet Mom.

Mom waved, quickly tucking her hand into her pocket. Snuggling close to me, she leaned in. "Chloe, I think I have more clues for your chart."

Why was I not surprised? If Mom's sleuthing could help solve this case, I was all for it, if she went about it safely.

"Anabel. Any more info about Lloyd's murder?" Mom blurted, drawing several pivoting heads in our direction. One lady covered her child's ears, glaring at Mom. It probably wasn't the time or place to discuss it. Sometimes I wondered if Mom didn't have a good barometer for situational awareness, or if on the other end of the spectrum she knew exactly what she was doing. Whatever her strategy, it usually proved fruitful.

Anabel stepped from my right to face Mom and me, closing the space to minimize others from hearing. She glanced around and slightly bent over, mostly in Mom's direction. "Not yet. This just might go unsolved."

"Oh, I don't think so," Mom said. Now I knew she had been off investigating. What in the heck had she been up to besides sprinkling her gnomes throughout the town?

With our observation of Greg and his sister at the restaurant, he remained at the top of my list. What could Mom have done to get more deets? Did she follow him somewhere?

"It's really sad it happened. I imagine Greg is stepping in to fulfill the Santa role?"

Anabel nodded as someone stepped to the podium and did another mic check. "Yes. He is for now."

"I almost hate to say it, Anabel, but from where I stand, Greg has the most prominent motive." My boy bumped my leg again. I peeked down at him to see if it was just from being jostled by the swarm. His head lifted to look at me. With his encouragement, I continued down the path on the topic of Greg. "Was he disgruntled from being ousted?" I would reveal the secondary motive of protecting his sister at the right time. Nobody else on my list was even near Greg's reasons. In my book, motive trumped all. If someone had enough incentive, they could find means and opportunity. I lacked those pieces of the puzzle, for now.

"Oh no. He would never do that," Anabel said.

Mom looked at me and slowly blinked, not buying the story either. Sometimes being too close to a situation blinded us to the reality. If Anabel knew anything, she kept tight-lipped. It hadn't previously occurred to me, but was it possible more than one person was involved? Anabel didn't appear to be in cahoots with Greg or anyone else. Her emotions at finding Lloyd seemed genuine. But was that an award-winning performance? Was there more going on behind the scenes?

CHAPTER THIRTEEN

How far could I press Anabel before she clamped up? Reviewing Max's and my chart of suspects in my head, I had so many more questions. Could I casually navigate the conversation to avoid it coming across like the third-degree? And why would she protect Greg if she was the person who influenced replacing him with Lloyd? My brain settled on Anabel moving to the bottom of the suspect list until any compelling evidence prompted a change. Time to move on to others.

"Do you know any reason someone would be upset with Lloyd?" I asked.

Mom elbowed my side, following my train of thought with the innocuous question.

"He was such a sweet man," Anabel sniffled.

The music volume decreased for what I assumed was preparation for the ceremony to begin. If we learned no more details before my sisters arrived tomorrow, we might never know the truth before we left Hollywerth.

I wanted to be wrong about Greg. And what I really wanted was for there not to have been a murder. But here we were. I forged ahead with more questions at the risk of Anabel shutting down.

An elbow struck my side again, more subtle this time. Mom coughed into her glove. Not so subtle. I waited, hoping Anabel would continue without me nudging. She turned, facing the enormous tree consuming the center of the gathering, gazing upward. The awkward silence not filled.

"Maybe Lloyd did something unknowingly to upset someone," I suggested. If I could keep the tone neutral and not accusatory toward Lloyd, maybe that would open Anabel up to consider other suspects.

"I suppose," Anabel said over her shoulder. "Nobody's perfect." She wiped her nose again, shaking her head. If I could only read minds, I might have a prospective direction to lead my questioning.

"I know parents can be awfully protective when it comes to their kids," I said. "Is it possible one of them confronted him about something he said to their child during their visit with Santa?" Massively reaching for straws, I wanted to exhaust all angles before

I would give up on this quest. If I had some detail that might be helpful to solve the mystery, I had to keep the onward movement. My responsibility gene came on strong to prod me in finding answers.

"Well," Anabel started. Was there a crack in the armor? Had I hit a glancing blow at the nail? "There was a complaint. But Greg had those too." OK. So a parent moved further down my suspect list. For now.

Venturing on to my next set of suspects, I said, "Change can be hard. Since Greg had been the Santa for so long, were any of the elves upset at the change?"

Swiftly pivoting to face me, Anabel held a finger up. "Look."

I took a small step back in the cramped space. My inquest looked like it had come to an end.

"All the griping from those guys didn't mean Lloyd was doing a poor job." She shook her finger at me for more of what appeared to be defensiveness of her decision to hire Lloyd.

"I'm sorry, Anabel." I tried to ease the tension for any last glimmer of a clue.

"No, I'm sorry to be so grouchy about this. Greg's time had come and gone to be Santa. He was good for a while, but I thought we needed fresh energy." She squeezed back into the small space on my right side, facing the tree. "I just don't know how I could have been wrong about him." Who was she referring to? Greg or Lloyd? Or someone else?

Mom's arm shot up and waved side to side. I stood on my tiptoes to spot who she was gesturing to.

"If I were you, I'd keep my eye on Greg, too," Mom said, grinning from ear-to-ear.

Greg and Jules huddled together on the exact opposite side of the crowd from us. Jules raised her hand and reciprocated Mom's greeting.

"Why do you say that?" Anabel sniped. I would think she would be more open to considering suspects. Though nobody wants to believe anyone they know could perform such a dastardly deed.

Glancing at Mom, I waited for her response. She opened the can of worms I wanted nothing to do with.

"Well," Mom started and stepped forward, her hand on her hip for emphasis. "It was more than losing the Santa job that might have sent him over the deep end."

Anabel looked at me.

I couldn't let Mom take the brunt of the message. "We overheard Jules and Greg talking at Bacon and Brews," I said. Was it really anything incriminating? Couldn't a brother be protective of his sister without it turning to murder?

"That woman spreads a lot of rumors. Frankly, I don't know how she stays in business," Anabel said. "Her stuff's not that good either."

Not true. Jules' treats were top-notch. "She seemed to think Lloyd was going to leave you."

There was no going back on this remark now. I shifted my weight from foot to foot, trying to stay warm, but also uncomfortable with the personal conversation with someone I barely knew. Her relationship drama was out on full display.

Shaking her head, Anabel said, "Not true. I know for a fact he had bought a ring."

"Was it for you?" Mom said, speaking my exact thoughts.

"Yes, it was Mabel. I have it on good authority. And it was a beauty too. Had my favorite stone, amethyst." Anabel held out her left arm, admiring the place a wedding ring would hold.

Well, if Lloyd wasn't interested in Jules, that mitigated Greg's motive for murder. Mostly.

Without prompting, Anabel answered my burning question. "My friend, the mayor, also owns the local jewelry store. Shelby even helped Lloyd pick out the ring for me. We were going to have a June wedding."

For a third time, Mom's elbow gouged my side. We needed another way for her to get my attention or I would wind up with a doozy of a bruise. I leaned over as she cupped her hand over her mouth, wondering what she could possibly know about the situation. I straightened up and shook my head after her suggested wild idea that might just crack the case wide open. If I could divert the conversation to another theory, I might be able to wrangle more details from Anabel.

"Are you sure?" I asked Mom. The more proof that corroborated Greg's innocence, the larger the hole became for the actual killer.

She pursed her lips and nodded. I knew that look well. When Mom asked you a question she already knew the answer to, you better fess up. This might be the only answer that made sense. I mentally reviewed the chart Max and I had created, shuffling the names on the list. Reluctantly, I moved Greg down. Even though I disliked him, and his motives were strong, the pieces just didn't come together to point to him for the murder. The more I thought about Mom's hypothesis, the clearer the picture became. Was I trying to force facts into a story, or were they revealing the killer?

CHAPTER FOURTEEN

"Sherrie!" Anabel hollered. The crowd noise escalated in anticipation just moments away from the big event. The time window significantly narrowed for gaining any more answers. Sherrie maneuvered her way through the mass of bodies to our side of the square, her head down as she squeezed through.

The music softened to indicate the festivities were about to begin as the mayor ascended the podium.

Sherrie quickly stole a glance at the tree as she wove through the last few rows of people to join us. Her face lifted to reveal her jowls sagging, sad during the most festive time of the year.

"Are you OK?" Mom asked, holding her hand out to Sherrie to pull her over the curb.

Sherrie shrugged and turned away from us. "As good as can be expected."

"I thought you might not make it," Anabel said.

"Was that your plan?" Sherrie said, her hands clenching along her side.

Mom slightly moved back as the tension between Sherrie and Anabel grew. "Hey," came a voice from behind us. "You stepped on my foot."

"Sorry," Mom said, returning to my side.

What in the world were they talking about? Whatever it was, it didn't seem to put Anabel in a very good light. But the dynamic certainly explained what Mom had whispered to me a few minutes ago.

"I'm glad you're here now," Anabel said in a sickly sweet voice, appearing to make up for whatever wrong she had done to Sherrie.

Sherrie crossed her arms, having none of it.

"I didn't have a choice," Anabel continued.

"You did," Sherrie replied. "You knew exactly what you were doing."

Would we have enough time before the ceremony began for this conversation to reveal what they were really talking about? Only mere minutes and the window might close shut on any more clues.

"Without Lloyd, I needed someone to work extra so we could open the gift shop on time," Anabel said.

Mom's head whipped toward me, her eyes bulged. Anabel's statement confirmed Mom's theory. Or at least advanced it as a leading candidate to explain all of this. Mom grabbed my arm and gestured like she was writing a note. I dug in my pocket for the piece of paper Max and I had worked on. Mom dug in her purse for a pen and grabbed the paper. She scribbled a few things, crossed some out, and drew several arrows. Max jumped up and put his nose on the paper, weighing in on this fresh development.

Sherrie pivoted slightly away from Anabel, giving her the childish silent treatment.

"I am very appreciative, Sherrie," Anabel said.

The tension between those two was beyond the employer-employee relationship. Hollywerth was a small town. And I knew all too well there were few secrets in a place like this since most everyone knew each other, quite like a large dysfunctional family.

"Ladies and gentlemen," boomed the announcer, standing at the mic next to the mayor.

If we were right, a killer stood right next to us. If we were wrong, there would be no returning to Hollywerth after a false accusation.

Mom flung her arm toward the podium as the police chief joined the mayor. Yes, getting this new information to the authorities was the best strategy. It would be out of our hands. Mom bent over and pried her way through several people, attempting to reach Thomas. She had the best chance of making her way through, so I maintained my position.

Silence ensued between Anabel and Sherrie. All eyes geared toward the massive evergreen about to be lit up so brightly it could probably be seen from space.

Max whimpered next to me as Mom continued weaving her way to the front of the crowd. I suspected he thought she was on another mission to hide more of her gnomes.

I reached down and put a hand on his back, feeling his pulse race, attempting to calm his anxiety.

The announcer introduced Mayor Shelby Cahill, and she approached the microphone. To her left, just offstage, a slight commotion prompted everyone's look as my mom scrambled up to talk with Thomas. Her hand was outstretched with the piece of paper that had all the scribbled notes for clues.

Thomas looked at the crowd and back at Mom.

She tapped the paper and pointed our direction. Would he attribute this encounter to a feeble, senile old lady? Thomas draped his arm around Mom, listening intently as she chattered on.

The mayor graciously asked for our forgiveness until they could straighten the matter out. Her tone was kind, but her look to Thomas said, *Get this handled now.*

Thomas attempted to escort Mom from the stage, but she didn't budge. Little did he know when her mind was set, there was little you could do to alter it. He nodded and followed Mom down the steps. Had she convinced him to come over to us? Or was he just humoring her to get her off the stage and out of the mayor's limelight? Either way, he had to delicately manage the situation between two strong women.

Mom grabbed Thomas' hand and navigated her return trip to our location. Would this confrontation be all for naught?

Max fidgeted to my right, unable to see the entire scene playing out.

Sherrie's head swiveled around. No way Thomas could arrive in time, especially with Mom in tow. I felt like I was watching a slow-motion movie and the criminal was moments from getting away.

Not to be denied, Mom barreled her way in front of Thomas, creating a path like a football blocker. About twenty yards from us, Mom yelled, "Don't let her get away!"

Sherrie ducked and shoved a woman to her left, causing several people to topple onto each other like dominoes. She wouldn't likely get far, but she might cause a lot of havoc in her attempt to flee.

Mom squealed like she was on an amusement park ride, now about ten yards to our right.

Like a lightning streak, Max flew to follow Sherrie. She turned just in time to catch him with her open arms.

"Max," I yelled.

Sherrie put Max on the ground, grabbing his collar and dragging him behind her.

He was no stranger to taking down killers, but could he wrangle his way out of this predicament? Mom and Thomas had gained speed as the crowd parted for them.

Spinning back in our direction, Sherrie yelled, "Back off or you'll never see the dog again."

I held my hands up in defeat, unwilling to chance harm coming to my boy. We had been through so much together. I couldn't lose him. Even if it meant letting Sherrie get away.

Sherrie inched backwards with Max trailing her. Was he compliant, just waiting for a lull to escape? Glancing at my boy's face, he appeared calm. Always sensing a step in advance, what was he anticipating would happen?

Mom quickly gained on Sherrie, Thomas bringing up the rear. "Mabel," he yelled. "Let me handle it." He attempted to overtake Mom, but she swung her elbow at him. He had no idea how lethal that thing could be when she connected.

As if we were watching an episode of the keystone cops, Mom reared back, ready to swing her large bag toward Sherrie.

CHAPTER FIFTEEN

With the full force of an Olympic hammer-throwing champion, my mother whaled her bag at Sherrie. Sensing a tremendous blow descending upon her, Sherrie cowered, hugging Max even tighter. At least she had stopped her egress through the crowd that now tightened around her. Sherrie wouldn't be making it out of here, but would she do any damage to Max in her desperation?

Mom connected dead on and Sherrie stumbled, releasing Max. He landed on the ground with all the grace of a cat, appearing to be unhurt. A massive amount of gingersnaps was due for my boy tonight, with lots of extra pampering. Max whipped his head around, not sure which of the gnomes that had spurted out of Mom's bag he should grab first. He grabbed the one nearby and pranced over to Mom, depositing it at her feet. He glanced around and gathered up the remaining wayward creatures and returned them to Mom. Was this a truce between them for now?

Sherrie scrambled to her feet, attempting to squeeze through the crowd. Mom had slowed her just enough so that Thomas could reach her before her escape. He extracted handcuffs from his pocket and slapped them onto Sherrie's wrists. I wondered if cops always kept those handy, even when they were off duty.

"You don't understand," Sherrie wailed as Thomas grabbed her upper arm, guiding her away. "I had to do it."

Apparently Sherrie watched little crime TV to know you shouldn't be yapping your jaw without an attorney.

Above the din of the crowd, as the Christmas music continued to play in contrast to the scene, Anabel sniffled next to me.

Thomas further guided Sherrie away as she blurted, "He was telling kids Santa wasn't real!"

"C'mon. Let's go," Thomas said.

Sherrie wriggled against his force. "This is Hollywerth. You just don't do that." She wasn't wrong. But why would she resort to such an extreme measure for a philosophical difference?

Planting her feet for one last outburst, Sherrie bowed her head, glaring directly at Anabel. "You," she spat. "He told me he would never leave you. He had only been leading me on."

Anabel lost it, leaning into me. I wrapped an arm around her. Not only did she lose the man she loved, but it was at the hands of the person she thought was a friend.

Thomas and Sherrie exited the scene as the mayor attempted to regain some semblance of order. How in the world do you recover from that ordeal to carry on? Someone pumped up the volume of music to turn the focus back on the event we were all here to watch. The mayor led the group singing "O Christmas Tree." How fitting. This town didn't miss a beat in their celebration.

Max trotted alongside Mom as they returned to my side, partners in crime solving. The two of them kept me on my toes. And I wouldn't trade either for anything.

Mom leaned against me, this time with a gentle elbow nudge. I squeezed her tight. "What do you think, Chloe?"

I was proud of her, but wanted to tread lightly for the wrong kind of encouragement. Smiling, I said, "You did great, Mom."

The music waned as the mayor took her position to direct the tree lighting.

"I think so too. What do you think about opening a side business when we get back home?"

As if running the treehouse hotel and opening a restaurant wasn't enough. I needed to discover her secret for the fountain of youth.

"Gumshoe Grannie. I think it has a nice ring to it." She hugged her purse as Max sidled up to her, the last gnome still wedged in his mouth.

"Ladies and gentlemen. Kids of all ages," the mayor forged ahead. Certainly, the lead up the ceremony was nothing short of a circus.

"We'll see," I replied to Mom.

"The moment you have all waited patiently for," the mayor continued, with a short story about the origin of the Christmas tree in anticipation of the lighting.

"I do have all of that sleuthing experience when you kids were at home." No doubt she had skills to detect what we had been doing while she was at work. As a single mom most of the time, despite the multiple marriages, her skills to scout out our antics were nothing short of professional. She could tell if something was out of place and had become an expert at reading us. From as far back as I could remember, there were never any secrets that hadn't come to daylight. I had learned early not to try to outsmart her. But my sisters and brother learned many lessons the hard way.

The mayor finished her story and had her assistant standing by at the switch to turn on the lights. She drew out the introduction, creating quite the anticipation. A few in the crowd grumbled to get on with the show. Ignoring the hecklers, she took the opportunity to highlight some of the custom-made ornaments decorating the tree that were made by local Hollywerth residents. With the anxiety of the crowd increasing, she took the hint and pointed to her assistant, holding up her hand for the countdown.

Mom giggled, covering her mouth, enjoying every second. Her infectious laugh got me going, too. Even Anabel smiled, despite all the drama from earlier.

A bump to my leg prompted me to gaze down at Max. I wondered if the excitement had finally gotten to be too much for him. We could all use a quiet time back in our suite.

From between Mom and me, Max somehow found a space to escape and beelined to the top of the platform, heading toward the mayor.

"Excuse me," I said, heading to corral my pooch. "Max!"

As he does when he is on the trail of something, he completely ignored me.

Not to be deterred from this last step in the lighting, the mayor headed to the switch, putting her hand on it.

"Max!" I hollered again as he disappeared under the tree. I fully expected him to emerge with another gnome. I had lost count of the number he had rescued, sure that his mission would continue our entire trip. Likely, he kept finding the same ones as Mom redistributed to different locations.

Not wanting to disturb the mayor, I skirted around to the back of the tree, peering around people to spot my boy. A kind woman holding a child pointed to her left. I followed her direction to locate my wayward dog, ready to forgive him given all that he had been through.

Thankfully, the mayor forged on, finally leading up to what we had all been waiting so long for. "Count with me, will you?" she said. "5-4-3-2-1."

The lights came on to a roar of cheers, the most spectacular tree I had ever seen. Rockefeller Center held nothing on Hollywerth for the Christmas celebration.

Spotting a buff-colored tail wagging at the back of the tree, I bent to see what Max had discovered, fully expecting a gnome. We were in for a second surprise of our trip.

Twitch Upon a Star

Chloe was basking in the glow of the Christmas tree lighting ceremony, and the satisfaction of solving the murder of Santa. Her thoughts turned to the arrival of her sisters the following day and getting on with the purpose of this family trip. However, the gift someone left under the tree was worse than a bag of coal.

Another murder mystery in the midst of this Bavarian-style village threatened to throw the entire small-town into mayhem. No sooner had her sisters arrived, than one of them threatened to leave, blowing up the entire family business plan. Playing the tourist, and shopping for answers, Chloe quickly generates a list of several suspects, topped by the star-studded mayor herself.

Can Chloe and her savvy spaniel sleuth out this mystery? Or will they be forced to forgo the family legacy? Find out in book 2 of the Murder All the Way Christmas Cozy Series.

ABOUT THE AUTHOR

S ue Hollowell is a wife and empty nester with a lot of mom left over. Finding a lot of time on her hands, and as a lover of mystery novels, she began telling the story of a character who appeared in her head.

One thing led to another and the Treehouse Hotel Cozy Mystery series was born. Through this experience she has discovered a love of writing stories, and especially mysteries. She hopes you enjoy her books as much as she enjoys writing them.

Sue misses her spaniels that passed, but they live on through her cozy stories. She loves cake, and the more frosting the better!

You can follow her Facebook for the latest news.

Printed in Great Britain
by Amazon

27770084R00058